The Little Red Hen

Susanna Davidson

Illustrated by
Daniel Postgate

Reading Consultant: Alison Kelly
Roehampton University

Map of the farm

Farmhouse

Hen house

Duck pond

Once upon a time,
there was a
little red hen.

She lived on a farm in a
little white hen house
with a bright red roof.

5

A glossy
black cat

who lived in the
farmhouse.

A big noisy duck who lived on the pond.

And a fat brown rat
who lived in the barn.

One morning, the little
red hen walked to
the field.

Hide! It's the
little red hen.

She was looking for
juicy worms to eat.

10

She went scratch, scratch, scratch with her small sharp toes

and she found some grains of wheat.

"Ooh!" she cried. She fluffed her feathers.

"Cluck, cluck, cluck!"
12

"Not I," said the cat.

"Not I," said the duck.

"Not I," said the rat.

"Fine!" said the little red
hen. "Then
I'll do it
myself."

And she did.

The little red hen pecked at the ground and made a hole.

One by one,
she dropped
the grains in.

The little red hen waited
for her wheat to grow
all through the
winter.

First, the shoots were small and green.

By spring, the shoots
were tall and strong.

In summer, they turned from green to gold.

At last, the wheat
was ready.

"Who will
help me cut it
down?" said the
little red hen.

"Not I," said the cat.

"Not I," said the duck.

"Not I," said the rat.

"Fine!" said the little red hen. "Then I'll cut it down myself."

And she did.

She cut down the
wheat without
any help at all.

"Who will help me take the wheat to the mill?" said the little red hen.

"I want to grind it into flour."

"Not I," said the cat.

"Not I,"
said the duck.

"Not I," said the rat.

She took the wheat
to the mill

and ground it into flour,
without any help at all.

"Who will help me make the flour into bread?" said the little red hen.

"Not I," said the cat.

"Not I," said the duck.

"Not I," said the rat.

"Then I'll make it myself," said the little red hen.

And she did.

She baked the bread
without any help at all.

"Who will help me eat the bread?" said the little red hen.

The cat, the duck and
the rat jumped up.

"Mmm," they said, as they smelled the bread.

The bread was warm and soft.

39

"I'll eat the bread,"
said the cat.

"I'll eat the bread," said the duck.

"I'll eat the bread," said the rat.

"Oh no you won't!"
said the little red hen.

43

"I'll eat it ALL BY MYSELF!"

And she did.

The little red hen's guide to making bread

First she gets:
450g (1lb) (3½ cups) strong white
bread flour
½ teaspoon salt
½ teaspoon sugar
2 teaspoons dried easy-blend yeast
or 1 teaspoon dried rapid rise yeast
300ml (1 cup) warm water
2 tablespoons olive or vegetable oil

When the little red hen reaches step
8, she heats her oven to 220°C,
425°F, gas mark 7.

1. First, she sifts
the flour, sugar
and salt through
a sieve into a large
bowl. Then, she
stirs in the yeast.

2. The little red hen
then mixes the
water and oil. Next,
she pours them into
a hollow in the
middle of the flour.

3. She uses a
wooden spoon to
mix everything
together until
she's made a
soft dough.

4. Then, she
puts the dough
onto a floury
work surface
and kneads it
for 10 minutes.

5. Next, the little red hen puts the dough into a clean bowl and covers it with plastic foodwrap.

6. She leaves the bowl in a warm place for 1½ hours. The dough rises to twice its size.

7. She kneads the dough for a minute to get rid of any air bubbles. Then, she puts the dough in a buttered loaf tin.

8. The little red hen leaves the dough for an hour in a warm place. Meanwhile, she turns on her oven.

9. She puts her loaf on the middle oven shelf and leaves it to bake for 35-40 minutes.

10. She leaves it to cool on a wire rack. Then she eats it all by herself!

Ask an adult to help you!

The Little Red Hen is an old, old folk tale.
It has been around for hundreds of years.
No one knows who first told it, but it
probably came from Russia.

Series editor: Lesley Sims
Designed by Louise Flutter
Cover design by Russell Punter

First published in 2006 by Usborne Publishing Ltd., Usborne House,
83-85 Saffron Hill, London EC1N 8RT, England. www.usborne.com
Copyright © 2006 Usborne Publishing Ltd.